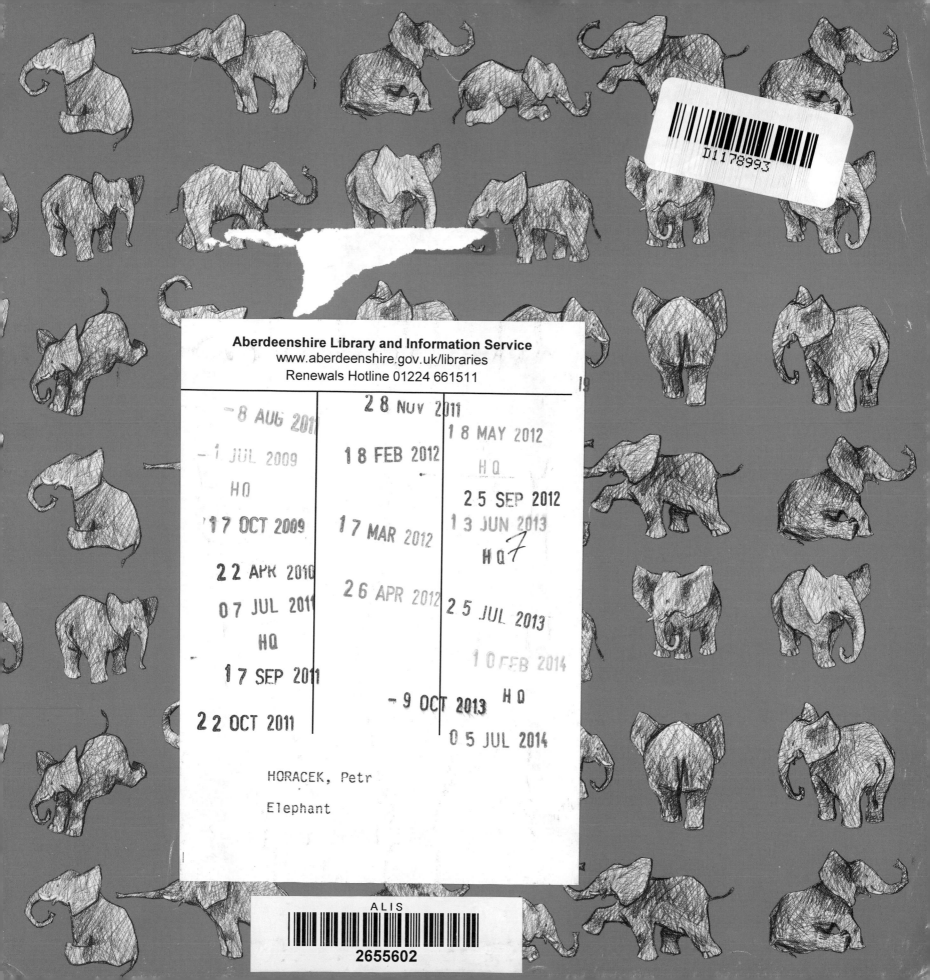

To Marin, Vincent and Max

E LEP

First published 2009 by Walker Books Ltd, 87 Vauxhall Walk, London SE11 5HJ   10 9 8 7 6 5 4 3 2 1
© 2009 Petr Horáček The right of Petr Horáček to be identified as author/illustrator of this
work has been asserted by him in accordance with the Copyright, Designs and Patents Act 1988
This book has been typeset in Horáček Printed in China All rights reserved. No part of this book
may be reproduced, transmitted or stored in an information retrieval system in any form or by any
means, graphic, electronic or mechanical, including photocopying, taping and recording, without prior
written permission from the publisher. British Library Cataloguing in Publication Data: a catalogue
record for this book is available from the British Library ISBN 978-1-4063-1100-6
www.walker.co.uk

Petr Horáček

HAN t

WALKER BOOKS
AND SUBSIDIARIES
LONDON · BOSTON · SYDNEY · AUCKLAND

I asked Grandad to play football
with me, but he was too busy.

I went to
see Grandma
but she was
busy too.

So I
asked my
ELEPHANT
if HE
wanted
to play
with me.

We played football
in the garden.

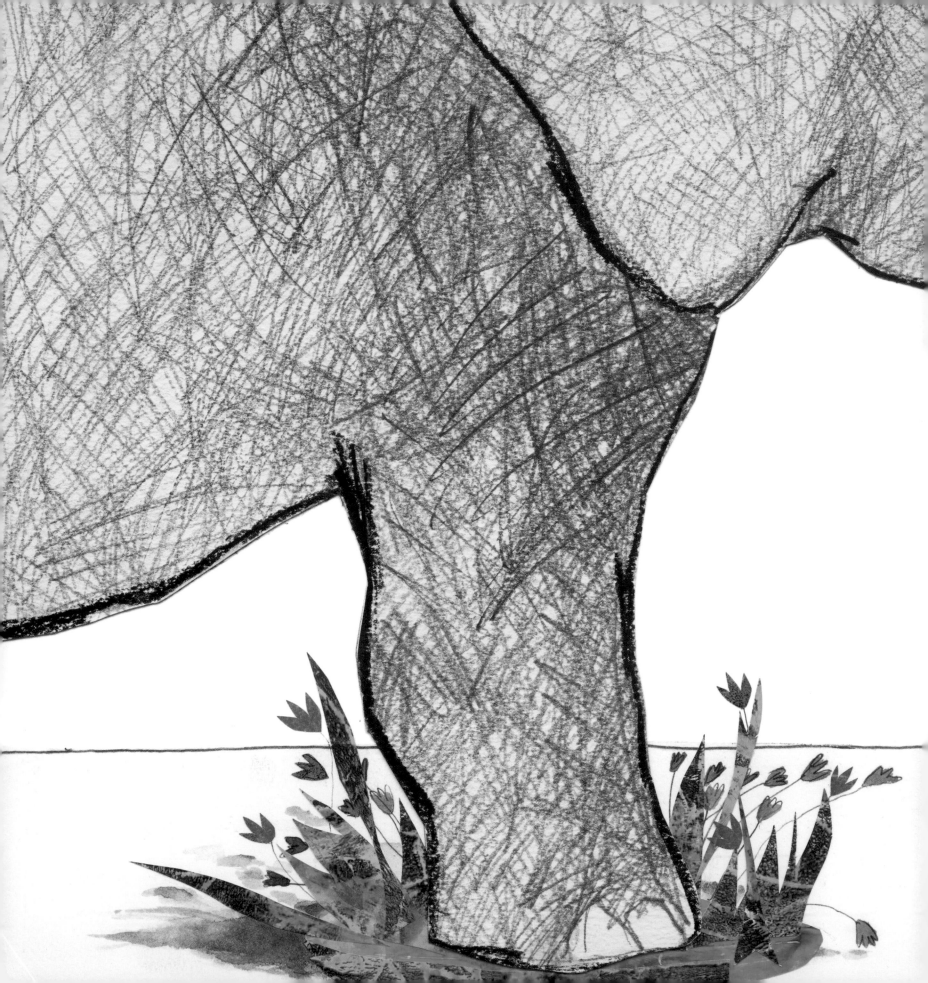

Then Grandad called, "Who MESSED UP the flowerbed?"

"I'm sorry, it was my ELEPHANT," I replied.

Grandad did not believe me,
so I took ELEPHANT inside.

Then Grandma called,
"Who MESSED UP the hallway?"

"I'm sorry, but it must have
been my ELEPHANT,"
I replied.

"And was it your
ELEPHANT
who

SPLASHED

and

made

puddles

in the

bathroom?"

"Was it your ELEPHANT who KNOCKED OVER the orange juice?"

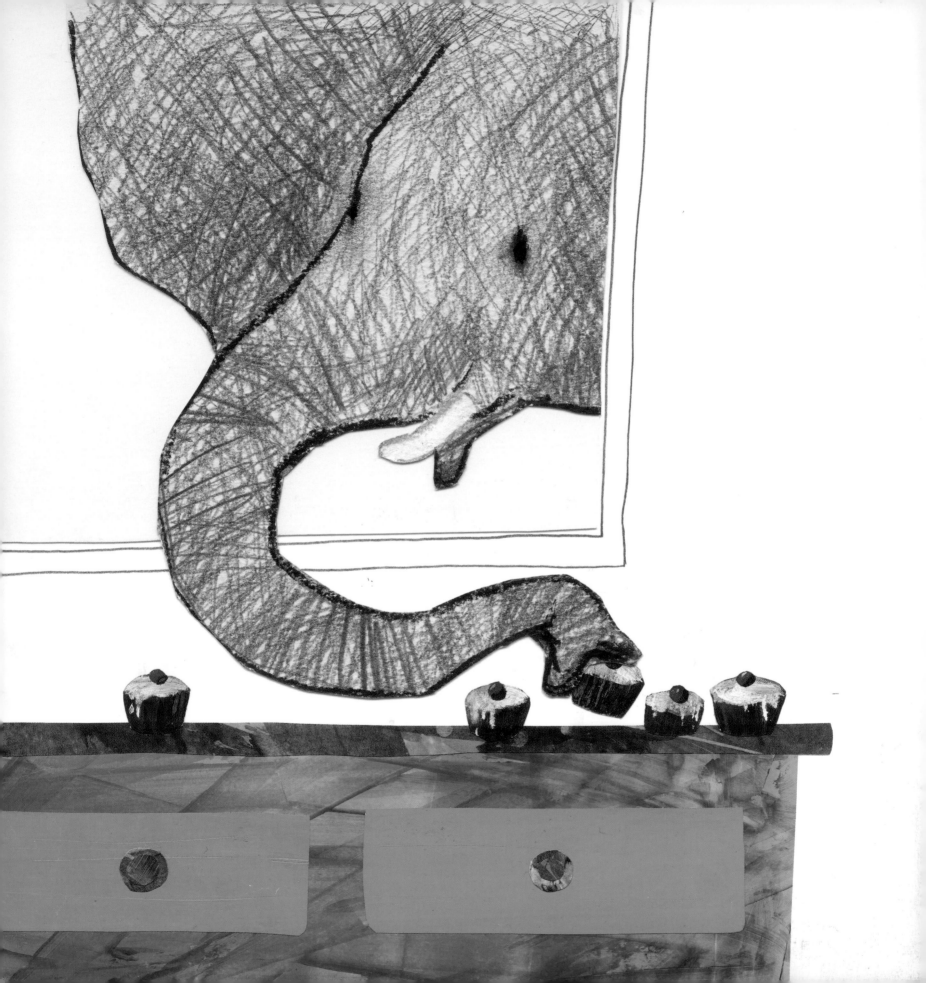

"And was it your ELEPHANT who ATE some of the cakes?" Grandma asked.

"Well ... yes," I replied truthfully. Grandma looked at me as if she didn't believe me.

I was upset.

I wanted

to be

alone.

Then my ELEPHANT came. He smiled at me. I said sorry for telling on him.

We were friends again.

We played in my room all day.

We went fishing. It was fun.

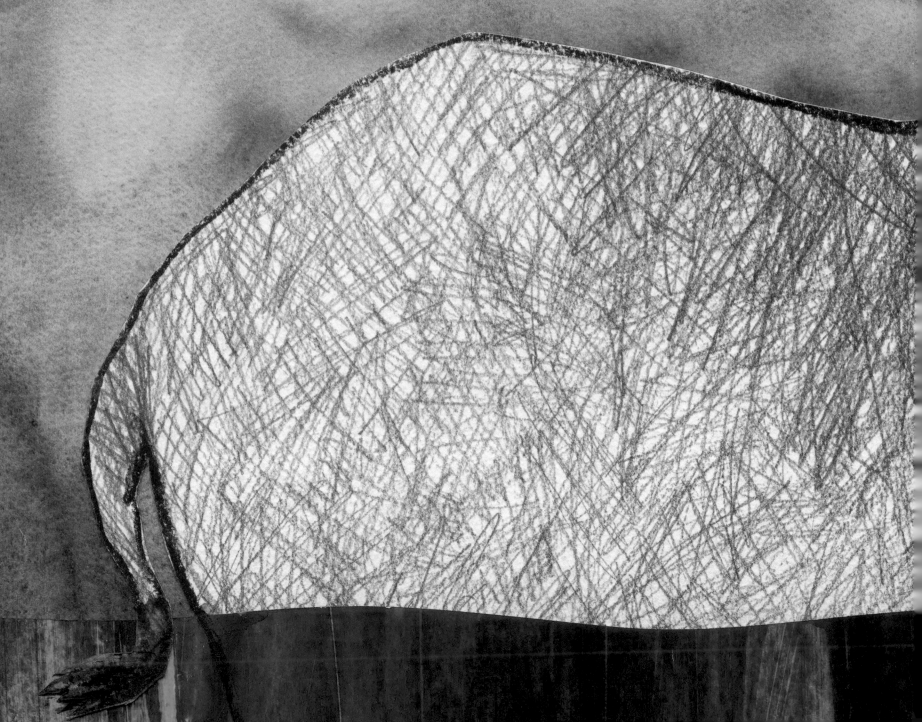

Then my ELEPHANT took me to
the jungle to see tigers until ...

it was
morning
and
Grandad
wanted
to play
football.

"But how did I get to bed?" I asked.

"You were tired..."
said Grandad.

"So your ELEPHANT took you to bed!"

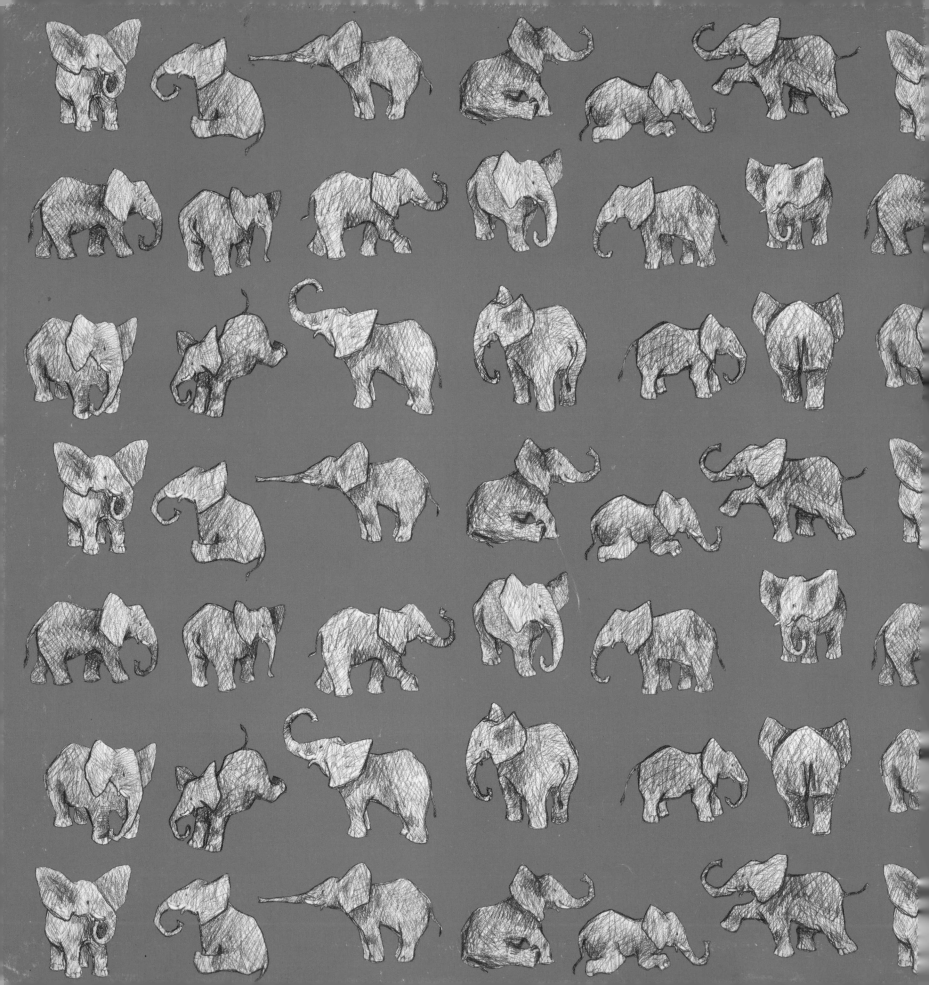